All rights reserved / CIP Data is available.
Published in the United States 2009 by
Blue Apple Books
515 Valley Street, Maplewood, NJ 07040
www.blueapplebooks.com
Clamato® is a registered trademark of Mott's LLP.

Distributed in the U.S.
by Chronicle Books
First Edition
Printed in China

ISBN: 978-1-934706-66-4

1 3 5 7 9 10 8 6 4 2

pOppy's Pants

by mElissa conrOy

blue apple books

For the real "pOppy"
& for Lila

-m.c.

Meet pOppy, who always wears khaki pants.
He spends many hours at his desk writing something.
He must have a lot on his mind.

pEnelope is pOppy's granddaughter.

Her favorite color is yellow, but she'll wear any color.

pEnelope likes to sew.

One day, pOppy asks pEnelope
if she would sew up the hole in one of his pairs of khaki pants.
She smiles and takes the pants from pOppy.

She puts the pants on the kitchen counter and
opens up the biggest, widest drawer in the kitchen,
the drawer that has everything in it.

pEnelope finds rubber bands, nuts and bolts, a dried piece of yellow clay, and a few black plastic things. Finally, she finds the sewing kit.

pEnelope looks at the assorted colors and decides
to ask pOppy his opinion.

pOppy's door is big and closed. So, pEnelope knocks.
At first, she is quiet. Then she is loud.
Finally, she decides to open the door a little bit.
She sees pOppy sitting in his red leather chair
with a glass of Clamato juice on his desk.

"Yep?" pOppy answers.

"What is your favorite color?" pEnelope asks.

"When I look at colors, what I see is different from most people.

I'm color blind, just like a cocker spaniel."

"O.K., pOppy," says pEnelope.

pEnelope imagines what a puppy's favorite color would be.
She remembers how they like to swim.

She looks at the selection
of thread colors again.
She decides that a puppy
would probably like
aquamarine best.

pEnelope threads
a needle and
starts sewing.
Then she discovers
a problem.

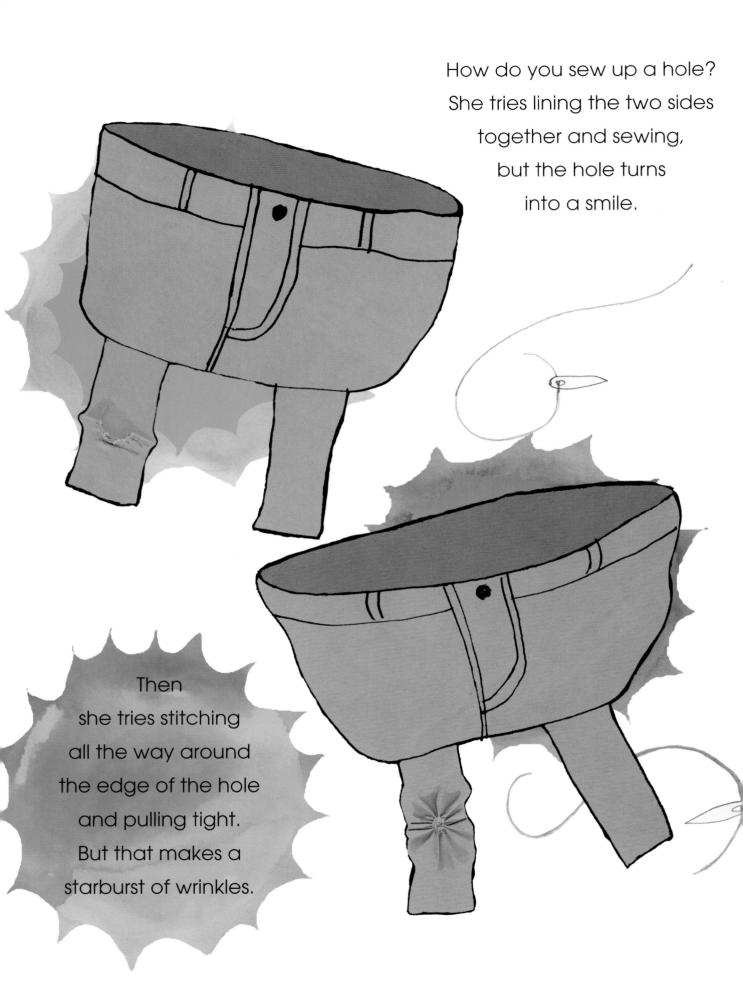

How do you sew up a hole?
She tries lining the two sides
together and sewing,
but the hole turns
into a smile.

Then
she tries stitching
all the way around
the edge of the hole
and pulling tight.
But that makes a
starburst of wrinkles.

pEnelope throws the pants on the ground
and jumps up and down on them.

she feels better.

pEnelope picks up pOppy's pants and brings them to her mAma.

"mAma, can you iron these pants for me, please?"

pEnelope takes
the freshly pressed pants
back to her work area
and studies the hole.

Finally, she decides
what to do.

pEnelope sews back and forth across the hole, from side to side,
and up and down, until almost all of the thread is gone.
The hole becomes an aquamarine web.
pEnelope beams.

She shows her mAma.

"Oh," her mAma says. "Good job!"

Then she goes to pOppy's writing room.

This time pOppy's door is open.

"Here you go pOppy," Penelope says.

"Thanks, pEnelope. What color is this?"

"Aquamarine, pOppy. I think cocker spaniel puppies would like it."

pOppy holds his new pants up for a better look. He gives pEnelope a wink.

"Good choice," he says.

pEnelope stands next to pOppy's chair while he takes a sip of
Clamato juice. Then he clears his throat and looks at the book on his desk.

Finally, pEnelope says,
"My favorite color is yellow."

"Why?"
pOppy asks.

"Because yellow is like the sun or a lightbulb.
Yellow gives me ideas and makes me happy," says pEnelope.

That evening, pOppy puts on his newly mended khaki pants
and makes a delicious dinner for pEnelope and her mAma.

After dinner,
they walk to the ice cream
parlor for some
rainbow sherbert.

The End

Thank you for reading pOppy's pants

Featuring:

pEnelope
She loves sewing,
drawing, and the smell
of strawberries.

mAma
She grows her
own herbs and spices
and enjoys riding her bike
in the wintertime.

pOppy
He enjoys being alone
to write and thinks
an extra scoop of bacon fat
improves the flavor of just
about anything.

sEymour
He's the puppy pEnelope imagines
will be hers one day.
She thinks he'll enjoy swimming with her.

What do you enjoy doing?

pOstscript

My second daughter, the comely and serene Melissa Conroy, is the artist who created this book for the pleasure of children. When she was a child herself, Melissa noticed everything and wanted to know how everything worked. Since I knew how nothing worked, she tired of me easily. But she made things, sewed things (including my pants), and even played a part in my own emerging career as a writer.

My wife, Barbara, presented me with the fresh copy of my book, *The Water is Wide*, typed by a professional. It looked terrific to me, and it came at the end of a long, hard struggle for my family. The Woo (a nickname I'd given Melissa) came up to ask me if she could borrow a piece of paper to draw on. Distracted, I gave her permission to do so. Later, however, I went into my office and noticed that the first page of my freshly-typed manuscript was missing.

"Woo? Woo?" I called out. I'd been tearing about the house for several hours when I remembered her request for a piece of paper.

I found her in the backyard drawing a butterfly, but she was using a different sheet of paper than the one I sought.

"Woo, this is important," I said. "Where did you put that piece of paper you borrowed from Daddy's office?"

"Lost it," she said.

"Lost it? Where?"

"If I knew the answer to that, Daddy, it wouldn't be lost," she said.

The first page of *The Water is Wide* was never found, and I had to rewrite it from memory. The picture of the butterfly, however, was the best Woo had ever drawn. Since that day, we have covered our walls and rooms with paintings and wall hangings and textiles that Melissa has created during her career. Melissa Conroy gave her family a great gift—we got to watch an artist grow up, and we have loved every minute of it.

pat cOnroy

Melissa Conroy started sewing
in second grade to repair her stuffed animals.
It was around that time that the real pOppy gave
her a pair of his khaki pants to mend.

She started making woOberry™ dolls when her daughter
gave her a "mAma" drawing with a baby in her belly.
Since then, Melissa has developed a line of characters,
each with their own story to tell. She sits down daily to draw and paint
with her daughter, who is now six and her son who is two.
Both have contributed drawings to this book.

To learn more, visit:
www.wooberry.com

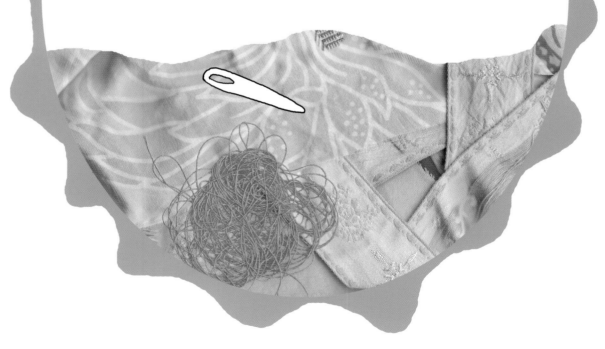

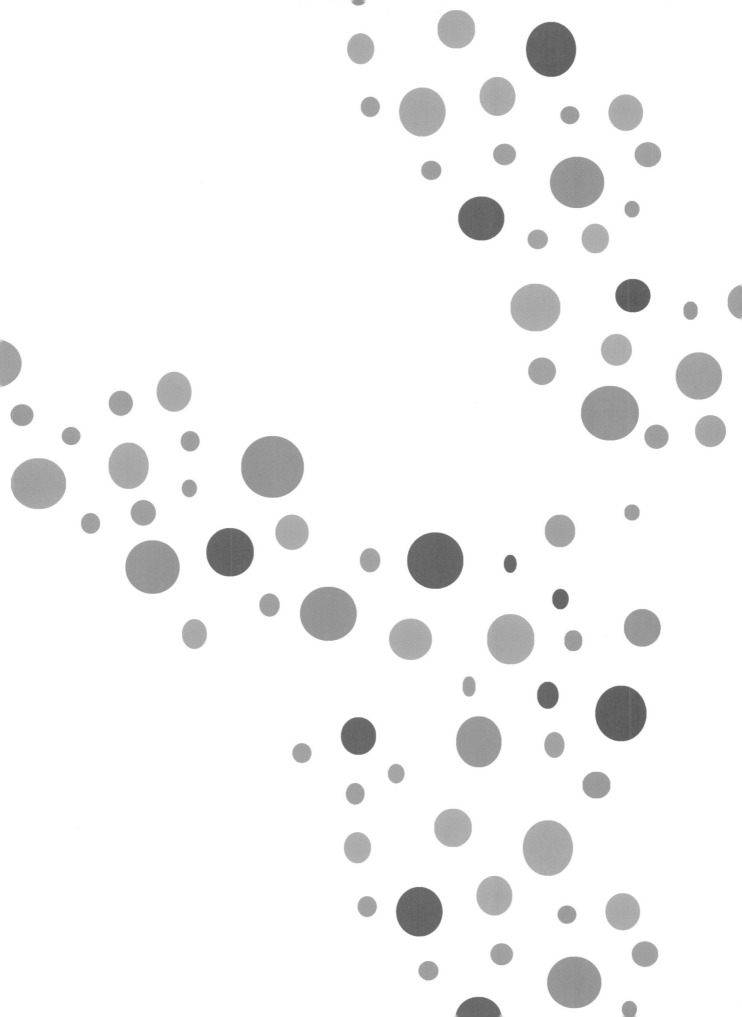

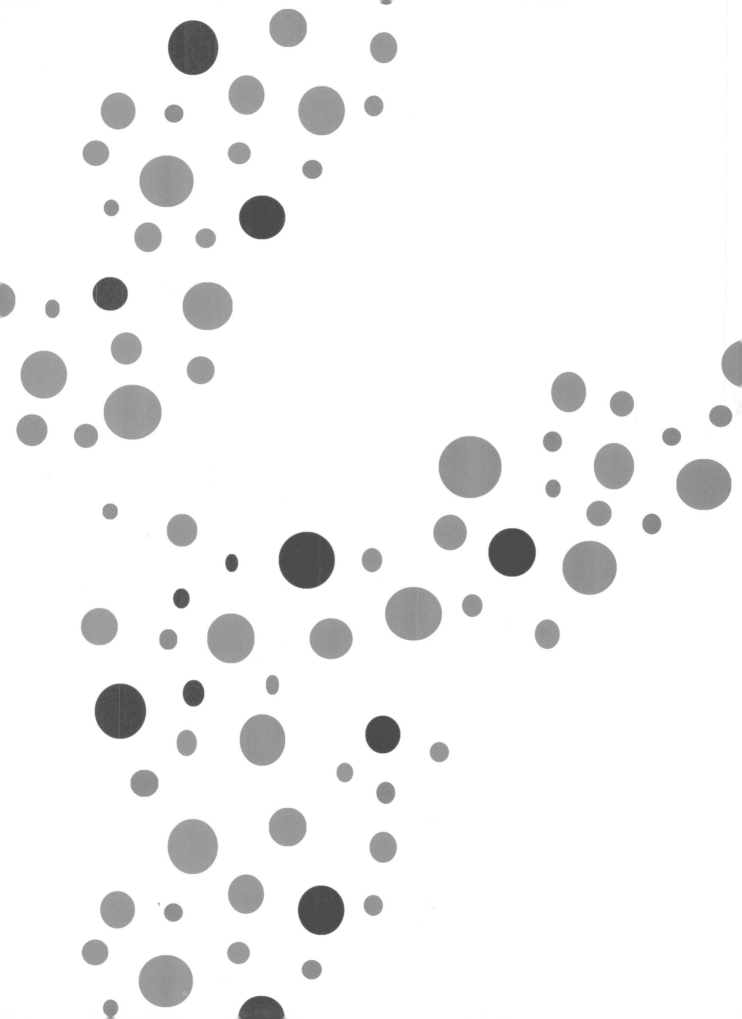